THE GREAT SNAKE

STORIES FROM THE AMAZON

SEAN TAYLOR

Illustrated by

FERNANDO VILELA

F
FRANCES LINCOLN
CHILDREN'S BOOKS

*For Dad – would I have written
this book without a father who loves
travelling, trees and chatting
with strangers? – S.T.*

For my wife, Stela Barbieri – F.V.

First published in Great Britain and in the USA in 2008
by Frances Lincoln Children's Books, 4 Torriano Mews,
Torriano Avenue, London NW5 2RZ
www.franceslincoln.com

British Library Cataloguing in Publication Data available on request

ISBN 978-1-84507-529-3

Illustrated with woodcut, Chinese ink and rubber stamps
Set in Adobe Garamond and Myriad

Printed in China
9 8 7 6 5 4 3 2 1

CONTENTS

> "Come with me into the damp thickness.
> The forest already knows someone has arrived
> and all its many greens shift, wanting to know who it is."
> *AMAZONAS: PATRIA DA ÁGUA*, THIAGO DE MELLO

I am in Brazil on a boat and we are setting off up the River Amazon. Ahead is the biggest river basin in the world. It contains one-fifth of all the fresh water on our planet. So much water floods out of the mouth of the River Amazon that it stains the Atlantic Ocean brown over a hundred miles out to sea. And surrounding the huge river is the world's biggest rainforest.

Our boat is called the Rio Afuá. Below deck the engines steadily chug, chug. Around me thirty or forty other travellers are slumbering in hammocks, playing cards, joking about yesterday's football results, or staring out across the water. Some of them are going to visit their families. Some are taking things to sell up-river. There are miners here hoping to find gold. And I have come because this is a place full of stories.

One of the first Amazon stories I ever heard was the legend of Jurutaí. Yesterday I was in a town called Abaetetuba talking to an old woman with quick, bright eyes called Dona Monte Serrat. I asked her if she knew the legend of Jurutaí. She nodded with a smile and started singing it to me. This is how the story goes…

THE LEGEND OF JURUTAÍ

Long ago, deep in the Amazon rainforest, there was a bird called *Jurutaí*. One night Jurutaí looked up through the warm air and saw the moon. The moon was perfectly round. Her silver light fell across Jurutaí's face as though she was reaching out to touch him. And Jurutaí fell in love.

Jurutaí fell in love with the moon and he wanted to fly to her. So he fluttered to the top of the tallest tree he could see. But the moon was still far away. He flew to the top of a hill. But the moon was still far away. So he flew into the sky. He flapped up and up until the air grew thin. But the moon was still far, far away.

Jurutaí flew on and up until his wings ached, his eyes stung and each breath seemed to fill his lungs with emptiness. He wanted to go on, but it was too hard. The strength drained from his wings and suddenly he was dropping. Down he twisted through the black air. Down he flapped. Down he fell, back to the damp, scented leaves in the trees. And he perched there, breathlessly blinking at the moon. She was too far away for him to reach. So all he could do was sing to her. Jurutaí sang the most beautiful song he could sing. He sang a song full of sadness and love and it rang out across the forest.

The moon stared down. She did not reply. And tears filled Jurutaí's eyes. His tears dropped to the ground. They rolled across the forest floor. They flooded valleys and flowed towards the sea. And people say that this was how the River Amazon was formed.

There is still a bird called the Jurutaí living in the Amazon rainforest today. Sometimes, when there is a full moon, it looks up at the sky and sings.

And I have heard of native Brazilian people who light fires when the full moon shines, and they sing and dance to encourage the jurutaí to sing. They know that singing the most beautiful song you can sing is the best way to get rid of sadness. And they believe that we should all light fires in our hearts when the jurutaí inside us falls silent.

It is morning now and I am looking out from the Rio Afuá across acres of water. The river is a great brown mirror. In it I can see the blue of the sky, the white of the clouds and, far off, the green of the forest. Perhaps a quarter of all living species in the world live here in the Amazon. There are spiders as big as baseball caps. There are monkeys which weigh little more than chickens' eggs. There are frogs which moo like cows. There are fish which jump two metres out of the water to snatch beetles off branches. There are butterflies so bright that you can see them a mile away.

Sometimes I think the people here tell so many extraordinary stories because they are surrounded by so many extraordinary creatures. Sometimes I think it is because so much mystery lies in the water and the rainforest. Scientists know more about the moon than they do about parts of the Amazon. Sometimes I think it is to do with the unique mix of people who live here – native Brazilians who have inhabited the forest for over 10,000 years, Europeans who first arrived from Spain and Portugal 500 years ago, and Africans shipped to South America as slaves. Their stories have mixed, like paints, to make new colours. The next tale is an example of this mix.

THE TORTOISE AND THE VULTURE

A vulture was perched near the top of a *tucumã* palm, munching at some tucumã palm fruits. Then he heard a voice. "Hey! Comrade vulture!" It was a tortoise.

"Comrade vulture!" repeated the tortoise. "You can get up there but I can't, so be a friend and throw me down some of those palm fruits."

The vulture peered at the tortoise with his stumpy legs and merry little eyes. Then he yanked off a clump of palm fruits and croaked, "Here! You can have one of these! But keep the rest for me!"

PLUMPF! down came the fruit and *NYAK! NYAK! NYAK!* the tortoise started gobbling at them. He gobbled and he gobbled. He gobbled until he had eaten every last one.

* * *

It wasn't long before the vulture swooped down.

"Eh?" he croaked. "Where have my palm fruits gone?"

"I put them down that hole to keep them safe for you," nodded the tortoise.

The vulture blinked a mistrustful sort of blink.

"I'll go and fetch them," said the tortoise, and he vanished down the hole.

Down he went, and he didn't come back.

"Hey! Tortoise! Out!" snapped the vulture.

But the tortoise didn't come out.

"I know exactly where my palm fruits are!" croaked the vulture. "They're in your belly! Now, out you come!"

But the tortoise didn't come out.

The vulture blinked again. This time it was a cheerful sort of blink. He could see the very tip of the tortoise's tail sticking out. In a flash the vulture jutted out his beak and bit the tail.

"Got you by the tail!" he said.

"You think that's my tail?" called back the tortoise. "That's a root!"

"It's your tail," said the vulture.

"It's not," said the tortoise. "Hit it with a stick if you want, and see if it makes me shout!"

That sounded like a good idea, so the vulture went to find a stick. But when he got back, the tortoise and his tail had disappeared right down the hole. The vulture narrowed his eyes and jabbed his head as far down as it would go. He thought he could see the tortoise's merry little eyes, but he wasn't sure.

"Where are you?" he croaked.

"Can't you see me?" asked the tortoise.

"Almost," said the vulture.

"If you want to see in the dark, you have to open your eyes wide," the tortoise told him.

That sounded like a good idea. So the vulture opened his eyes wide.

"Can you see mc now?" asked the tortoise.

"No," said the vulture.

"Then open your eyes wider!" called the tortoise.

The vulture opened his eyes as wide as he could. And the tortoise flicked earth into his face. The vulture's scraggy neck yanked back and the tortoise took his chance. He scurried off as fast as his stumpy legs would carry him. By the time the vulture had stopped blinking, the tortoise was safely hidden in the undergrowth. And they say that the vulture is still chasing after him to this day…

The sun set over the forest several hours ago and I am sitting at the front of the Rio Afuá as we push on through the night air. Around me, the forest is like a great bowl of darkness. But the night is not all dark. I can see a swarm of stars above me and the moon just over the branches of the trees. Every now and then an explosion of lightning, far across the forest, punches one side of the sky full of light.

At the front of the boat, a searchlight scans the water for sandbanks, and floating tree-trunks. Occasionally another boat's light appears and disappears upstream. And, where the river meets the forest, there are hundreds and thousands of fireflies winking tiny, green-white dots of light.

There is an old ship's welder on board called Senhor José de Deus. During the day some of us were sitting at the front of the Rio Afuá, enjoying the breeze coming in off the river, and Senhor José de Deus started telling a story. It was about a character who is half-woman, half-fish – an Amazon mermaid. In Portuguese she is known as the Mãe d'Agua, which means 'Mother of the Water'. This is the story Senhor José de Deus told…

17

THE MOTHER OF THE WATER

They say that a young woman called Graciela was setting off on a journey up the River Amazon. She was pregnant and on her way to visit her mother in a small town called Monte Alegre.

Graciela boarded the boat with her bag and her hammock and as she did, a woman dressed in white walked past. The woman was beautiful. Her eyes were the colour of sea-water when sunlight shines through it. Her hair was long and black. As she passed, she looked into Graciela's face.

"You will not finish this journey," she said. "You are going to drown."

The young woman stared at the stranger.

"But… how… what do you mean?" she asked. "How can you know?"

"You will see," said the stranger. And she turned away.

Graciela's face was pale with fear. Boats along the Amazon are often overloaded. Every now and then one of them overturns and the passengers are drowned.

"Wait…" she called out. "Isn't there anything I can do to save my life?"

"There is one thing you can do," said the woman. "Promise you will give me your baby once it is born."

Graciela's chest rose and fell. She wondered if she would really have to keep the promise. How would the woman ever find her again?

"If it means I'll arrive safely, I promise to do it," she said.

"Then your life is safe," said the woman. "And, when it is born, you will give me your baby." With that, she walked off across the deck of the boat.

* * *

On the first night of the journey there was a storm. Even the crew was scared that the boat would roll right over. But it didn't.

* * *

Graciela's mother hugged and kissed her daughter when she arrived safely in Monte Alegre. And some days later a baby girl was born.

Weeks passed. The baby girl grew. Graciela tried to put the strange woman out of her mind. As the weeks became months, she thought about her less and less. Then, exactly seven months after the birth, she woke at dawn and there was the woman in white, standing in her room.

"It is time now," she said.

The room wasn't big enough for the shriek that Graciela let out. "NO!"

But the woman in white had already picked up the baby. In a flash she was out of the house, running with quick, light steps towards the river.

Graciela dashed after her – but not fast enough. The woman in white reached the riverbank and, without breaking her stride, she dived, with the baby girl under one arm. In a splash she was gone.

The young mother knew that she would never see her daughter again. She knew because when the woman disappeared, her feet were not feet any more. They had become a tail – a fish's tail.

from where I am sitting the Amazon looks like the sea. It's more than ten miles wide here. In front of me is nothing but a flat expanse of water soaked in sunlight. After three days with the clatter of the boat's motor in our ears and the swaying wooden deck under our feet, we are arriving at a town called Santarém. The last time I made this journey was eight years ago. That was when I first heard talk about a gigantic snake living in this river. The snake is supposed to be thirty metres long. She appears at night with eyes shining like the headlamps of a lorry, and she is so big that she can overturn boats. They call her the Cobra Grande, 'the Great Snake'.

In Santarém eight years ago, I got talking to an old fisherman who was mending his nets. I asked him if he had ever seen the Great Snake. He told me, "Only twice. The first time she came out of the river so close to my canoe that I could see her teeth. They were as long as my arm from the fingers to the elbow. The second time she swam after me and sent up a wave so big that my canoe was thrown right up on to the river bank."

No one believes everything old fishermen tell them! But at least half a dozen people since then have told me they have seen the Cobra Grande. Stories about her are heard right across the Amazon. This is one that I like…

THE GREAT SNAKE

One afternoon, close to where the River Trombetas flows into the River Amazon, a young woman called Zelina was washing in the water. As she splashed her face, she felt something brush against her legs. She didn't see what it was, in fact she didn't think of it again. But time passed and she discovered she was pregnant. Nine months later she gave birth to twins, a boy and a girl. But when Zelina saw the twins, she almost fainted. They were snakes! Can you imagine?

Zelina was terrified.

"What can I do?" she sobbed.

There was only one person she could think of who might help – the old medicine-man who lived in the forest. He knew more than anyone about plants and animals.

Zelina's body was heavy with worry as she walked through the trees looking for the medicine-man. He was crouched near his hut and, when he saw the snakes, he called out, "Throw them into the river! Throw them back into the water where they come from!"

This broke Zelina's heart, because she had no other children. But that night she named the boy Norato and the girl Maria-Caninana. Then she went to the river and threw the snakes into the brown water.

* * *

Years passed. The twin snakes lived wild and free in the river. And they grew. They grew five metres long. They grew ten metres long.

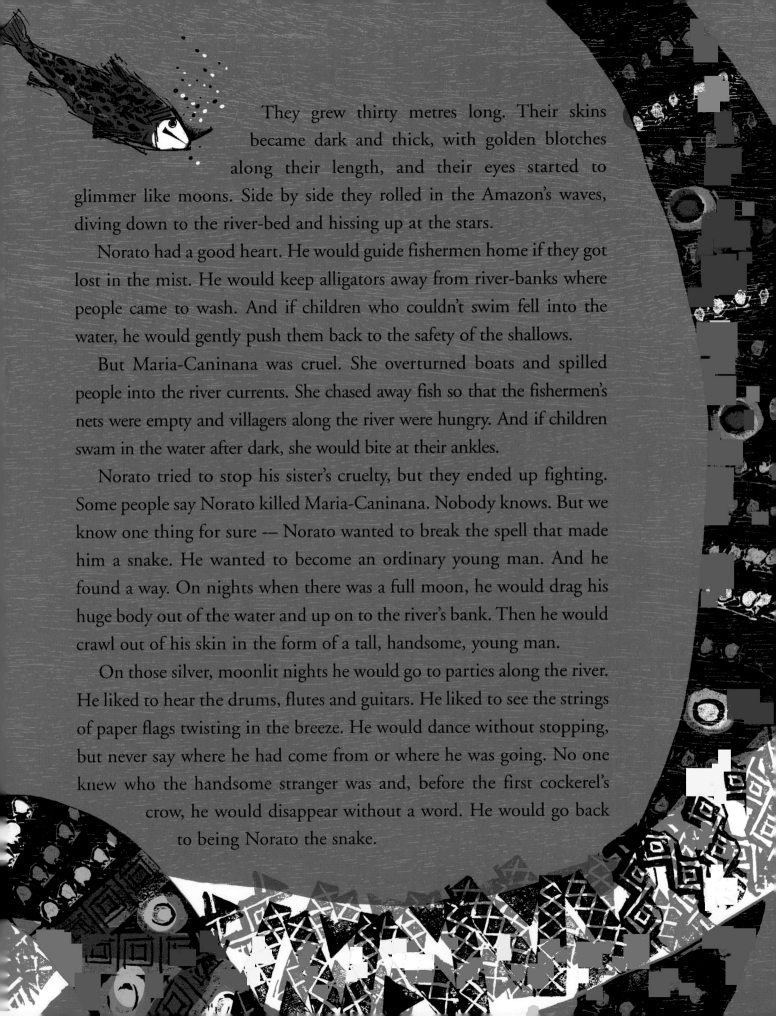

They grew thirty metres long. Their skins became dark and thick, with golden blotches along their length, and their eyes started to glimmer like moons. Side by side they rolled in the Amazon's waves, diving down to the river-bed and hissing up at the stars.

Norato had a good heart. He would guide fishermen home if they got lost in the mist. He would keep alligators away from river-banks where people came to wash. And if children who couldn't swim fell into the water, he would gently push them back to the safety of the shallows.

But Maria-Caninana was cruel. She overturned boats and spilled people into the river currents. She chased away fish so that the fishermen's nets were empty and villagers along the river were hungry. And if children swam in the water after dark, she would bite at their ankles.

Norato tried to stop his sister's cruelty, but they ended up fighting. Some people say Norato killed Maria-Caninana. Nobody knows. But we know one thing for sure -– Norato wanted to break the spell that made him a snake. He wanted to become an ordinary young man. And he found a way. On nights when there was a full moon, he would drag his huge body out of the water and up on to the river's bank. Then he would crawl out of his skin in the form of a tall, handsome, young man.

On those silver, moonlit nights he would go to parties along the river. He liked to hear the drums, flutes and guitars. He liked to see the strings of paper flags twisting in the breeze. He would dance without stopping, but never say where he had come from or where he was going. No one knew who the handsome stranger was and, before the first cockerel's crow, he would disappear without a word. He would go back to being Norato the snake.

This went on for many months. Then, at one of the parties, Norato saw the old medicine-man from his mother's village. The medicine man knew who he was. He greeted the young man by his name, and Norato realized this was his chance to find out something he longed to know.

"Tell me," he asked the medicine-man, "is there a way that I can remain a man for ever?"

"Norato, there is a way," the medicine-man told him. "You must find someone and take them to that snake-skin you leave on the riverbank. They must hit it hard enough to make it bleed, and pour a few drops of milk between its teeth. Then... *PFFFFFFF!* The skin will disappear and you will be a man for ever."

* * *

The first person Norato asked to help him was his mother. Zelina went with him to the river, but when she saw the gigantic snake, she froze. Memories of the twin snakes filled her mind, and she would not step down on to the shore.

Norato asked other people. Some laughed. Some said they were too tired. Some said they didn't have time. One man agreed to go and he stepped down on to the shore. But the snake's huge teeth and staring eyes stopped him in his tracks. He wiped a finger through the sweat on his forehead and said, "I'm not going near that. Find someone else."

Norato tried. He travelled on up the river and one night he stopped in a town called Cametá. He made friends with a soldier and asked if he would help. The soldier was not afraid. He walked straight up to the snake and hit it with an axe. *CRO! CRO! CRO!* Blood trickled out. The soldier put milk between the snake teeth. And at once the gigantic skin turned to ashes, which blew off across the river.

Norato was a man at last.

* * *

What became of Norato after that, no one knows. But every now and then you hear stories about someone getting stranded along the River Amazon. A handsome young man appears. He shows them the way, or fixes their boat. The young man will never say where he is from, or where he is going – only that his name is Norato.

And what about his sister, Maria-Caninana? Well, some people believe that she is still alive. They say she is the Great Snake that appears in the night with eyes like the headlamps of a lorry, terrifying people up and down the river.

Now I am in the small town of Santarém. It is very hot. We are almost on the equator. The sun hammers down. It is the kind of heat that makes dogs lie down with their legs in the air!

A lot of people here get 'motorbike taxis' rather than walking. The rides are cheap, and you don't arrive where you are going soaked in sweat. If you walk, you stroll along very slowly. So this feels like the moment for a story I have heard about the slowest of all rainforest animals – the three-toed sloth. It is a kind of shaggy-dog story, or rather, a shaggy-three-toed sloth story.

A LONG WAY TO GO

Far off in the forest, Three-Toed Sloth looked up into the branches of a *taperebá* tree and saw three plump taperebá fruits. They were just beginning to turn from green to yellow. And plump taperebá fruits are good to eat when they are yellow.

Three-Toed Sloth was hungry. So off he went, climbing up the tree. But he was slow… he was so very slow that the taperebá fruits turned yellow, and Three Toed-Sloth still had a long way to go.

* * *

Three-Toed Sloth carried on climbing. But he was slow… he was so very, very slow… that one of the taperebá fruits fell off the branch, and Three-Toed Sloth still had a long way to go.

* * *

Three-Toed Sloth carried on climbing. But he was slow… he was so very, very, very slow… that a second taperebá fruit fell off the branch, and Three-Toed Sloth still had a long way to go.

* * *

He was getting near the top, and there was one taperebá fruit left. It was plump. It was yellow. It looked so good to eat. But Three-Toed Sloth was slow… he was so very, very, very, very slow… that just as he stretched out a slow hand on the end of a slow arm… the last taperebá fruit dropped to the ground.

"Oh for goodness sake!" puffed Three-Toed Sloth, looking at the three tamerebá fruits lying on the ground. "If I hadn't come racing up here in such a mad rush, everything would have been all right!"

So down Three-Toed Sloth went. He was looking forward to eating those plump, yellow taperebá fruits on the ground. But Three-Toed Sloth was slow… he was so very, very, very, very, very slow… that, when he reached the ground… the taperebá fruits weren't taperebá fruits any more. They had grown into taperebá trees.

On one of them there were three plump taperebá fruits just beginning to turn from green to yellow. And plump taperebá fruits are so good to eat when they are yellow…

It is raining now. As they say in Portuguese, Está chovendo canivetes, 'It's raining penknives'. Towers of rain billow and twist in the wind. Great heavy drops thud into the river and clatter onto Santarém's roof-tiles. Rain washes fish-scales, fruit pulp and warmth from the market paving. White water floods the gutters. Incredible bolts of thunder fill the sky. It is rain that lashes down and bounces back up into the air, rain that stops the boats, rain so heavy, you almost expect to see fish swim past through it!

All through this journey I have been watching dolphins rolling in and out of the river. These clever, playful animals are known as botos. Sometimes they appear on their own. Sometimes they come in twos or threes. Many people here are wary of dolphins because of the stories about them – stories of dolphins turning into handsome young men dressed in white suits. They visit the villages along the river and get up to mischief, always keeping their hats on so that no one can see the breathing holes on top of their heads.

Time for a watery story. Time for a dolphin story. This is one which is told around Santarém…

THE DOLPHIN AND THE FISHERMAN

One night, a fisherman called Joel was out on the river. Everything was still. Stars, reflected in the water, drifted this way and that. But there were no fish. Joel sat in his canoe with one hand on the end of his net, hoping to feel a tug. But no tug came. He pulled the net in, coiling it carefully at his wet feet. The net was empty. It had been empty all night. The only living thing he had seen was a big dolphin jumping out across the river. But Joel wouldn't catch a dolphin. People said catching dolphins brought bad luck.

* * *

Hours passed. The moon rose. There was silence except for the splash of Joel's paddle in the black water and, far off, the croaking frogs.

"What are my children going to eat tomorrow?" Joel asked himself.

Then the dolphin rolled out of the water. *SPLISH!* It was close to his canoe.

"Know what?" whispered Joel. "I'm going to harpoon that dolphin!"

He grabbed his harpoon and waited a minute or two. Then the dolphin appeared again. In a flash Joel threw the harpoon. *THUMP!* A hit. The dolphin twisted with a messy splash and tried to swim away. Joel gripped the harpoon rope. But the dolphin was so strong that the rope jumped from his hands into the river.

Joel groaned. He had caught nothing, and now he had lost his harpoon as well. But he wasn't going to give up. He dropped his net into the water again, hoping that something might turn up.

And something did turn up – another canoe, coming towards him. That was strange, so late at night. Even stranger, the man paddling the canoe was dressed in a white suit. He looked like some kind of foreigner.

"Excuse me, sir!" called the stranger.

"Hello!" Joel called back.

"Was it you who hurt my friend?"

"Your friend?" replied Joel. "No."

"Somebody hurt my friend," said the stranger.

"Not me," shrugged Joel. "I've been here on my own. I haven't caught a thing all night. I've only managed to harpoon a dolphin... and it got away."

"That dolphin *is* my friend," said the man.

Joel stared at the stranger. His head was full of tales of dolphins changing into men dressed in white.

"Look... I have children to feed," he said, fiddling nervously with his net. "I was desperate."

"Well, my friend is desperate," said the stranger. "He is at the bottom of the river with your harpoon in his back. We can't pull it free. Will you go down there and pull it out?"

"Go to the bottom of the river?" blinked Joel. "How?"

"Get in my canoe," said the stranger. "I will take you there."

Joel rubbed his thin cheeks. What would happen if he went off with this man? What would happen if he refused?

Right or wrong, he got into the other canoe and the stranger started rowing. They went faster and faster until, in the middle of the river, the stranger said, "Shut your eyes!"

The fisherman shut his eyes and felt himself dropping. The canoe spun headlong, endlong. There was a rush of water in his ears. The river's coolness washed over his head. He could taste mud in his mouth.

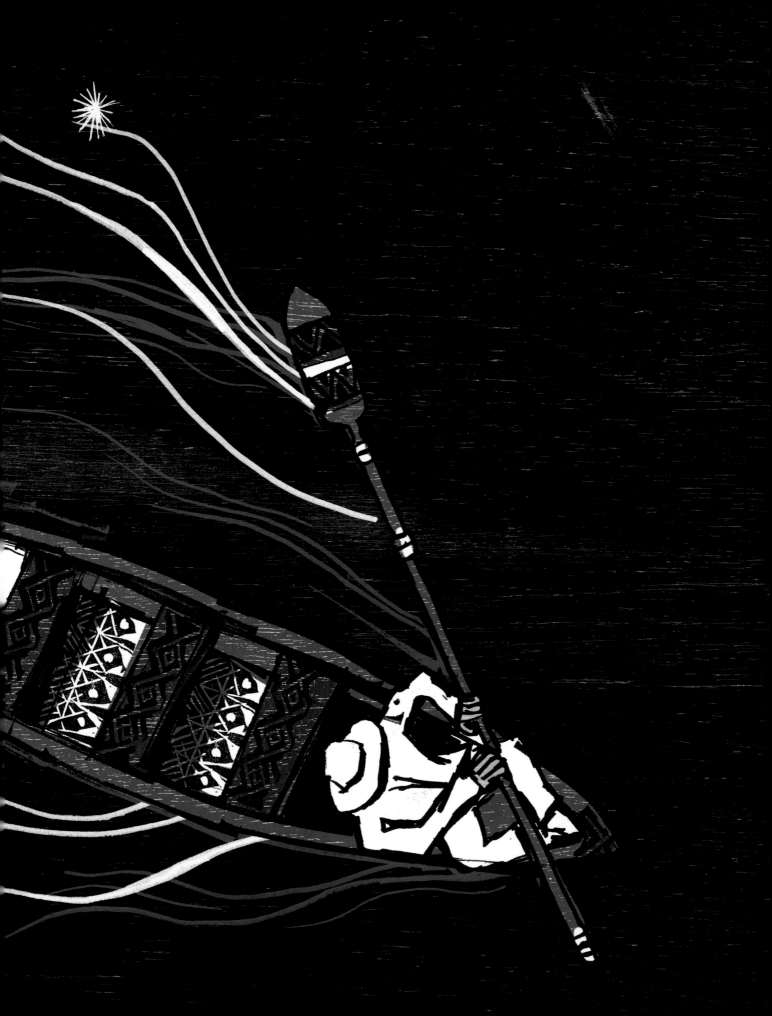

Then the stranger was saying, "Open your eyes."

Joel looked about. He was at the bottom of the river. He could move and breathe. Around him were little streets of bone-coloured houses. Overhead a sky of water stretched away. There were big fish, small fish and turtles swimming about in it like birds. And there was the dolphin, lying on a bed of weeds with the harpoon in its back. A shoal of silver jaraqui fish swam round it, tugging at the rope, but they were too small to pull the harpoon out. Joel got out of the canoe and took hold of the harpoon. With a tug, he pulled it free. Blood clouded the water. But the dolphin was all right. It flicked its tail and swam away.

"There," said Joel to the man in the suit, "now let's go back to my canoe."

The stranger smiled.

"I will take you if you agree not to harm our people again," he said.

"All right," Joel nodded.

"Good," said the stranger, and they got back into his canoe.

"Shut your eyes," he told Joel.

The fisherman shut his eyes, and felt himself rising. He could taste mud in his mouth. The river's coolness washed over his head. There was a rush of water in his ears. The canoe seemed to spin headlong, endlong.

* * *

He was back in his own canoe, in the middle of the hot night. His clothes were dry. He had his harpoon. There was no sign of the stranger. Everything was still. Joel looked down at the water, and he could tell that there were fish right by his canoe. He didn't hesitate. He threw his net in the river. And, when he pulled it in, it was heavy and gleaming, full of silver jaraqui fish – the ones he had seen at the bottom of the river.

Now I am two hundred miles further up the river. And I am in the forest. The ground is soft under my feet. The air smells of roots and leaves. Sunlight comes through the branches in a few long, straight rays. They touch thickets of palm trees, tangles of creepers and leaves the size of flags. Beside me, a tree rises so high that I cannot see its top.

It is quiet, but now and then I hear sounds. A hollow, woody call from an unseen bird. The thud of a tumbling fruit. A quick chatter of monkeys. A breeze in the leaves up above. Occasionally, the sound of something bigger pushing through undergrowth, far off.

The forest I am in stretches away for hundreds of miles in all directions. But it is getting smaller. We are destroying it. I have seen barge after barge heading downriver, full of tree-trunks which will be sold as timber around the world. And I have seen huge, grey-blue clouds of smoke spilling into the air where people are burning down trees so that they can use the land for farming and mining.

Destroying the forest isn't something you can turn on and off like a light switch. Millions of people live here. These are their stories I am retelling. Most of them use the forest to make their living. They have no choice. Like all of us, they use what nature gives them to survive.

But I ask myself, who has a better life if the forest is destroyed? Who has a better life if the forest is left standing? Why do some of the Amazon people choose to protect the forest rather than burn it down? And what will future generations think of us if we do destroy it?

I love being here, but I don't feel comfortable. My face is sticky with sweat. There are leaves that sting, biting insects, trees with spikes which sink into skin like fishhooks. There are hundreds of species of poisonous snakes. There are jaguars. And the greatest danger of all is something very simple – it is easy to get lost. According to local stories, dozens of fantastic beings live here too. They bring to life the fierceness and the trickery of the forest. There is the mapinguari, a monster with a mouth in its belly. There is the matintaperera, a ghostly woman who comes as a gust of wind. And there is the curupira…

THE CURUPIRA

Watch out for the curupira! His body is covered with hair as red as blood. His teeth are green. And his feet are turned the wrong way round - so if anyone tries to follow his footprints, they go in the wrong direction.

The curupira is only the size of a boy, but he is dangerous. He loves the animals and the trees. When people go into the rainforest, he watches what they do. If they hunt animals to feed their families, or they cut trees to build their own houses, the curupira does not mind. But if they kill animals for pleasure, or cut trees to make money, he gets angry. And if the curupira is angry with you, then you are in serious trouble...

* * *

Once there was a man called Mundico. He lived in a town along the river Amazon, but he liked to go hunting deep in the forest. He knew a place where few people went. Some said it was a part of the forest protected by the curupira. They said to Mundico, "If you go there, you should leave a little tobacco or rum as a gift for him." But that made Mundico laugh.

"People just tell those stories because they're frightened!" he would reply.

One morning, Mundico took his rifle, fetched his friend Avelino and together the two of them set off hunting. The shadows grew, the light dimmed and the path disappeared. They pushed their way through great arches of leaves and palms into the moist, cool thickets of the forest.

Everything around the men was hushed, but shifting with life. And it wasn't long before they heard the light tread of a deer. They were after it at once, kicking through vines and jumping over fallen branches. Avelino was the first to get the deer in his sights. *BANG*. He missed. But a second shot came from Mundico. *BANG*. Down dropped the deer. If the men had just headed home with that deer, everything might have turned out differently. But they kept going.

They passed under towering trees with scarred sides and muddy wasps' nests bulging from their branches. They shot a pair of bony-legged spider monkeys from the canopy of the forest. They shot a *curassow* bird in its nest. They killed a wild pig hidden in a rotten tree-trunk, and grinned at its angry piglets as they scattered in different directions.

Then, through the half-light they saw a huge *sapopema* tree in a clearing. When Mundico and Avelino reached the tree, they put down their rifles. They built a fire, boiled coffee and sat against the high roots.

What the two men had shot was more than they could carry home. So, when they had drunk their coffee, Mundico lifted the deer on his shoulders and Avelino took the wild pig. They left the other dead

animals where they lay.

What they didn't know was that the sapopema tree was where the curupira lived. He had seen everything. And he was angry.

* * *

Mundico led the way back through fat-stemmed bushes and peppery leaves. Suddenly something caught his eye. It was a young jaguar. Mundico had always dreamt of arriving back in town with a jaguar on his back. He dropped the deer, ducked round a fallen tree and set off into the trees.

His footsteps were light and quick. There was the jaguar, padding through the shadows. Mundico raised his rifle. But the jaguar had gone. It appeared again in a thicket of creepers. But when Mundico aimed, it was no longer there. He ran to where he had last seen the animal. His breathing was fast and shallow. There it was, further on. But again, when he aimed, it vanished.

He touched his head and looked about. There it was, standing still. Sunlight lit its back. Mundico aimed and fired. *BANG*. The jaguar fell.

"Got you!" he yelled. But when he reached the place where the jaguar had fallen, it was not an animal he found. It was a man's body, lying dead on the ground – the body of his friend Avelino! Mundico dropped his gun. The colour drained from his lips. He looked about as if someone might be there to help. And there was someone. It was a small figure covered in red hair.

The curupira's teeth peeped from his smile.
His eyes were cold as marbles. But what made Mundico
really afraid was a sound: *KLUNG-ALUNG-GULUNG!*
It was the curupira's belly rumbling.

Mundico turned and ran. He stumbled between saplings, through
spiders' webs and roots. He ran without looking, without thinking.
And as he ran, he could hear that sound behind him,
KLUNG-ALUNG-GULUNG!

He ran on until sweat stung his eyes and ran in trickles
down his back. He could hear sticks cracking behind him,and
he ran, ran, ran until he could not run any further.

Then he slumped to his knees, looking round with eyes wide and white.

There was nothing. The curupira had gone. All he could see was a handful of monkeys in the branches. They were chattering, screeching and chucking twigs into the air.

Mundico blinked. He coughed. He got to his feet and wondered which way to turn. He walked one way and all he found were nameless streams stretching into the forest. He walked another way, but he kept coming back to the same bushes and the same trees. Mundico walked until the nerves in his legs trembled. He walked until darkness fell. He shouted for help. But no one heard. The only sounds were barks and howls in the night, and the endless sizzle of the tree crickets.

Mundico did find his way home. But it took three days, and ever since there has been sadness in his eyes because of what he had done to his friend. Some say that now, whenever he goes into the forest, he leaves a gift of tobacco or rum for the curupira. Others say that he has never set foot in the forest again.

For the last few days I have been in Barreirinha, staying with a Brazilian poet called Thiago de Mello. Yesterday we left Barreirinha in Thiago's small motorboat, and he brought me to a house he has built in the forest on the River Andirá. It is near a village called Freguesia. I am writing this on the veranda of the house. There are no other buildings in sight, just trees, the dark water of the River Andirá, and the old white-haired poet lying in a hammock, reading.

Thiago has many friends here. Earlier today, he introduced me to 84-year-old Dona Coló and her husband Senhor Feliz. When I asked them how many grandchildren they have, "Over fifty…" was the answer they gave. For much of the afternoon we sat round big pans roasting manioc pancakes in banana leaves.

Manioc is a root a bit like a potato. Right across the Amazon it is the main food people eat. There are several stories about how manioc roots were first created. This is one I have heard on this journey…

MANI'S MYSTERY

Many years ago, when the world was still young, there was a village deep in the rainforest. For some months each year, the people who lived there managed to find fruit and catch fish. During those months they had plenty to eat. But, every year, there were other, hard months when there was little fruit to find and even fewer fish to catch. The adults grew thin. The children's bellies ached with hunger.

Then, one day, something strange happened. The village chief's daughter, Mara, gave birth to a baby girl. But the girl was unlike any baby anyone had ever seen before. Her skin was white, like milk. Her hair was as pale as the light of the moon. They named her Mani.

Everyone in the village grew to love Mani. The small, pale girl did not eat or drink much. She spoke little. But she was beautiful and clever. Her face was full of smiles. She was always pointing up at the birds and the monkeys. When she ran around with the other children, she looked like a moonbeam in the middle of them all.

Years passed. Life in the village was still good when there was food, and still hard when the food ran out. Mani grew into a beautiful girl. But she would wander around as if in a dream. She would go off into the rainforest and stay there, staring up at the orchids in the branches and watching humming-birds.

Her mother told her not to go off on her own, but Mani paid no attention. At night, while everyone else slept, she wandered into the forest between tree-trunks which were darker than the darkness. She saw the moon through curtains of palm leaves, and listened to the night calls of the *buraqueira* owls.

One day, as Mani walked in the forest, she met a boy from another tribe. No one knows what they said to each other. But perhaps they fell in love, because a few days later Mani and the boy ran away. Mani's grandfather, the chief of the village, was furious. He sent a group of warriors to bring Mani back. The men found her, but she would not come. There was a fight. There was an accident. Mani was killed.

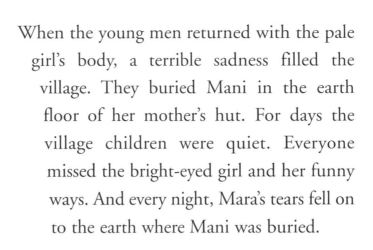

When the young men returned with the pale girl's body, a terrible sadness filled the village. They buried Mani in the earth floor of her mother's hut. For days the village children were quiet. Everyone missed the bright-eyed girl and her funny ways. And every night, Mara's tears fell on to the earth where Mani was buried.

* * *

Months passed. People began to put Mani from their thoughts. The children started chasing each other round the village again. Life returned to normal. But then something else happened. A leafy shoot appeared in the earth where Mani was buried. The shoot was unlike any plant anyone had ever seen.

The shoot grew and grew, until the earth around it began to crack. The chief of the village said they must find out what was underneath. So, with the villagers looking on, Mara dug into the dark earth.

45

Underneath, there was no sign of Mani. Instead, there were dozens of thick roots. Mara picked one and scraped it. It was as white as milk.

That night Mara dreamt that the moon spoke to her. The moon said, "Plant the roots that grew where Mani was buried. More will grow. Cook them. They will be good to eat."

So Mara planted the roots in the forest. Several months later, hundreds of other roots were breaking through the soil – and they were good to eat. The chief said, "We will name this plant after Mani. It will be called *manioc*."

And, from that day on, no one in the village went hungry again.

Yesterday I visited a school in Barreirinha and told the children some stories from my part of the world. As I was leaving, someone said that if I liked stories, I should go and visit Senhor Ignácio Lucas.

I met Senhor Ignácio later in the day. He was 84 years old, with thin arms, sun-dried skin and tufty black hair pushed back from his face. I found him in a wooden house on stilts, at the back of a compound where three or four families live. Outside the house was their barracão – a big kitchen area with a roof thatched from palm-leaves, like an open barn.

I spent most of the evening sitting at their long table. Senhor Ignácio's family drifted in and out, curious about the funny-looking visitor from another country. His wife Dona Angela was there, his son Raimundo and his many dark-eyed grandchildren.

There was a smell of years of wood smoke. Chickens came scratching round the plastic legs of my chair. Raimundo poured sweet coffee from a thermos, and it wasn't long before we were swapping stories, jokes and songs. They drifted in and out – a bit like his family.

I loved the way Senhor Ignácio told his stories. There was a sparkle in his narrow eyes, and when something made him laugh he threw back his small head, opened his mouth as wide as it would go and laughed with the whole of his body. This was the story his grandchildren asked him to tell…

I REALLY MUST BE GONE

Jaguar looked out of his den. He was hungry. He wanted to go into the forest and hunt. But he had his cubs to look after. Then Fox came past.

"Fox!" he said. "Will you look after my cubs? Then I can go hunting. I'll share whatever I get with you."

Fox agreed, and Jaguar slipped away between the bird-filled trees.

* * *

Before long, Jaguar had caught a big tapir. But he didn't share it with Fox. He ate it all himself. Then he went to sleep in the shade of some banana-palms.

Fox waited all day. The jaguar cubs grew so hungry that she had to feed them herself, and it was night when Jaguar came back.

"I didn't catch a thing," he sighed. "But let's do the same thing tomorrow. I'll share whatever I get with you."

So Fox stayed with the cubs. In the morning Jaguar went off hunting. Again he came back late at night. And although his belly was full, he pretended to Fox that he had not caught a thing.

"Never mind," he sighed. "Let's do the same thing tomorrow. I'll share whatever I get with you."

Fox stayed with the cubs, but she was suspicious. In the morning Jaguar went off hunting and when he didn't come back, Fox shook her head. She was not going to be tricked any more. She went on her way, leaving Jaguar's cubs on their own.

It was night when Jaguar returned to his den. He found his cubs wide-eyed with fear and hunger. And he was furious.

"Fox, you're going to pay for this!" he growled.

He thought of a plan to catch her. He knew where Fox lived. Nearby there was a field of *jamaru* gourds. The next morning, Jaguar went and hid there inside a hollow gourd.

When Fox came past, she could see a large bottom and a long tail sticking out of a jamaru gourd. And Fox had a pretty good idea whose large bottom and long tail they were. To make sure, she called out:

"Jamaru gourd! Tell me, is Jaguar hiding somewhere round here?"

Jaguar was taken by surprise, but he didn't make a sound.

"Jamaru gourd!" repeated Fox. "Tell me, is Jaguar hiding somewhere round here?"

Jaguar didn't know what to do.

"Jamaru gourd!" called out Fox. "If you don't reply, I'll run off."

There was nothing for it. Jaguar put on a squeaky, jamaru-gourd voice.

"No!" he said, "Jaguar definitely isn't hiding round here!"

"Hah!" shouted Fox. "There you are, Jaguar. You'll have to excuse me... I really must be gone!"

And she was.

Jaguar thought of another plan. He invited all the animals to a party the next day. Fox arrived late, and the party was already in full swing. Monkey was there with his guitar. Armadillo was there with his scraper. And Tortoise was there with his flute.

Jaguar seemed very pleased to see Fox. But she was careful not to get too close to him. Then Jaguar called out to the other animals:

"Come on! I want to dance with you, one by one!"

So the animals played and Monkey danced once round the den with Jaguar.

"*Twang! Twang!*" he went, "*Strum-strum-strum!*
Who will be eaten before the night is done?"

The animals laughed and cheered. Armadillo danced with Jaguar.

"*Ki-ni-ki-ni-ki!*" he went, "*Ki-ni-ki-ni-kep!*
Somebody here had better watch their step!"

The animals cheered even louder. Tortoise danced with Jaguar and he sang,

"*Fin, fin, fin! Fon, fon, fee!*
Jaguar wants a tasty little snack for his tea!"

There was more laughter, and Jaguar looked at Fox.

"Your turn," he nodded, reaching out a hand. "Come and dance."

Fox got up. She danced in. She danced out. She danced up. She danced down. But she danced just beyond Jaguar's reach. He tried to get close, but she was too quick. Every time he came towards her, she danced back.

"*Jaguar is angry!*" she
sang, "*Jaguar is strong!
But you'll have to excuse me...
I really must be gone!*"
And she was. Off she went, feeling
happy, as foxes sometimes are.
And, if Jaguar hasn't
caught her, maybe she
is still happy today!

I am on another boat, now. It is called the São Francisco. The river around me is full of the heat of the sun. It is the last day of my journey. Before long we will arrive in Manaus, the Brazilian city which sits in the middle of the Amazon forest.

Even while everyone was packing up their bags, there were stories in the air. I went to the front of the boat to escape the afternoon heat. As I stood there a big man with angry-looking eyes called Domingos took over the steering-wheel. I didn't think he would believe in the Great Snake or the curupira. Some people shake their heads and say, "Those are just stories." But two or three of us started talking, and soon Domingos was telling us that, after travelling up and down the river for seven years, he is sure the Great Snake is real. Then he described a lake where his family lives: "There's an island on it," he said, "a real island with rocks and sand, and it moves around the lake. One week it's here, then it's there!"

I looked at his face. He was serious, but smiling at the same time. I have grown used to that look. In the Amazon, people often laugh at their own belief in fantastic stories. But all the same, they believe the stories.

* * *

The buildings of Manaus came into sight. I headed off to take down my hammock. "There's another lake nearby," I heard Domingos say. "If you go there, you can hear the sounds of people living under the water. You can hear voices, you can hear drums, you can hear cockerels crowing at midday…"

With that in my mind, I set off into the city. And if you could see my face, you would probably say it was serious… but smiling.

55

About the Stories

These are not *the* stories from the Amazon. They are just a handful of stories I have come across while travelling through a small part of the huge forest. I found some of them in books and heard others told by storytellers. I have rewritten them in my language and in my own way.

THE LEGEND OF JURUTAÍ

The jurutaí is a real bird found right across the Amazon, and they do sing sad songs into the night sky. I first heard the legend of Jurutaí told by my friend, the Brazilian storyteller Giba Pedroza, in São Paulo. I heard another version sung by Dona Monte Serrat in Abaetetuba. It is originally a native Brazilian story.

THE TORTOISE AND THE VULTURE

When I was in Abaetetuba, I met a lovely old woman called Dona Nina Abreu. She had hard, dry hands and hair as white as wool. We swapped stories sitting at the front of her house, surrounded by the brightly-coloured traditional carvings of boats, canoes, birds and saints that she and her family make. One of the stories she told was 'The Tortoise and The Vulture'. It had her in fits of giggles!

THE MOTHER OF THE WATER

The Mother of the Water, or Iara, as she is sometimes known, features in many Amazon stories. In some of these, a young man is spellbound by her beauty and dives into the river to find her. Then he disappears or drowns. In others, like the story in this book, the Mother of the Water appears on land. Both Senhor Éfrem Galvão in Santarém and Dona Coló in Freguesia told me about actual encounters with the Mother of the Water. I heard Senhor José de Deus tell this story as we travelled on the *Rio Afuá*.

THE GREAT SNAKE

There are stories about the Great Snake told all over the Amazon. As far back as 1560 this creature was mentioned in letters written by early Portuguese settlers. I have heard variations of this story told up and down the river. I have also referred to versions in Luis Camara da Cascudo's *Lendas Brasileiras* (published in 1945), and in Maria do Socorro Simões and Christophe Golder's *Belém Conta...*(1995). This book came out of an amazing story-collecting project based at the University of Pará which did a lot to spark my interest in stories from the Amazon. I have yet to meet someone who has actually been helped by Norato, but when I asked Dona Coló about him, she told me, "Norato helps people."

A LONG WAY TO GO

I was told this story in Belém. I was visiting the offices of the Mamirauá Institute for Sustainable Development and had to wait for a rainstorm to pass. I started talking to a secretary called Dona Maria. As she organised the afternoon's post, and the rain came twisting down, she told me this story.

I have seen three-toed sloths in the forest. They often hang upside down from the branches of *embaúba* trees. Every day they spend around 18 hours sleeping. Their usual colour is light brown but, sometimes they turn green. Because they move so slowly, colonies of algae grow on them. I even heard about one found by scientists which had a mouse nesting in its fur!

THE DOLPHIN AND THE FISHERMAN

At least three people have told me about meeting river dolphins in the form of handsome men in suits and hats. I once heard this story when I was travelling on the River Negro and I have come across it in books, including *Nheengaré ou Paranduba Dos Dabacuris* by Moacir Andrade (1985) and *O Matuto Cearense e o Caboclo do Pará* by José Carvalho (1930). A recording of the story, told by a man called Francisco Bezerra, was published in a book called *Santarém Conta* by Maria do Socorro Simões and Christophe Golder in 1995. There are no records of any river-dolphin legends from more than two hundred years ago, so it is thought that the stories were first brought to the Amazon by Europeans.

THE CURUPIRA

Half the Amazon people I have asked about the curupira tell me he does not exist. Half tell me he is real. Tales of this fierce trickster may well have arrived with the very first native Brazilian tribes who settled in South America over ten thousand years ago. The tale I have written is based on a true incident I was told by a hunter called Vicente dos Santos. He took me into the forest one morning and told me about a man called Avelino who was shot by his own friend while they were hunting. The rumbling belly comes from an old woman I met called Dona Julienne. She made the *KLUNG-ALUNG-GULUNG* sound as she described seeing the curupira in the forest when she was a child.

MANI'S MYSTERY

This story comes from the Amazon's native Brazilians. It is a legend originally told by Tupi tribes. I first heard this version told by Senhor Éfrem Galvão in Santarém.

I REALLY MUST BE GONE

Senhor Ignácio Lucas told me this story in Barreirinha. Its structure is very African, but the slow-witted jaguar is a traditional character in Amazon folktales. The fox is more unusual. (There are no foxes in the rainforest.) Like other stories in this book it may have been passed from storyteller to storyteller for hundreds or thousands of years. I don't know who those storytellers were or where, or how they lived, but if they had not told these stories then this book would not exist. So I would like to end by raising my hat to those storytellers – whoever they were.

Glossary

algae – simple plants with no roots or leaves.

barracão – a living area for a family, open at the sides but covered by a roof.

botos – a kind of pink river dolphin common in the Amazon region.

buraqueira owls – small owls which live underground. In English they are called 'burrowing owls'.

canopy – the layer formed by the highest branches and leaves of the trees in the rainforest. Most of the animals in the Amazon live in the canopy.

curassow bird – a large bird, a bit like a turkey, found in the forests of South and North America.

curupira – the legendary protector of the forest, feared by many.

Dona – a way of saying 'Mrs' in Portuguese.

embaúba trees – fast-growing trees with thin trunks. In English they are known as 'trumpet trees' They have sweet fruit which three-toed sloths love to eat.

está chovendo canivetes – an expression in Brazil used to describe very heavy rain. It means, 'It's raining penknives'.

fireflies – small flying beetles which communicate with each other by making their bodies light up in the dark.

jaguars – large cats found in South America. They are usually a yellowish-brown colour with dark spots. Their jaws are strong enough to break open the shell of a tortoise.

jamaru gourds – large round vegetables with hard skins.

jaraqui fish – silver fish with stripy tails. A popular food along the River Amazon.

Jurutaí – a long-tailed, grey-brown bird which comes out at night. In the Amazon it is sometimes called an 'urutau', which means 'ghost bird'. In English it is called a 'common potoo'.

Mãe d'Agua – a mermaid who appears in many Amazon stories. People see her sitting at the edge of the river, singing or combing her hair.

manioc – a root vegetable which is the main food for people in the Amazon. Another name for it is 'cassava'.

mapinguari – a one-eyed monster said to live in the Amazon forest. It is gigantic, with long hair, sharp claws and a mouth in its belly. Bullets are supposed to bounce off its skin.

matintaperera – A harsh old woman thought to move in the form of an owl or a gust of wind.

native Brazilian people – the first people to live in what is now called Brazil. They are often referred to as 'indians'. Some native Brazilian tribes have never made contact with the rest of the world.

river basin – the area of land drained by a river and its tributaries.

sapopema tree – a tree with roots above the ground to support it. In English these are called 'buttress roots'. They can stretch 30 metres away from the tree's trunk.

scraper – a hollow, wooden percussion instrument played with a stick.

Senhor – a way of saying 'Mr' in Portuguese.

spider monkeys – acrobatic monkeys which almost never touch the ground. They can use their tails to hold on to branches.

taperebá tree – a fruit tree found in the Amazon. Taperebá fruits are called 'hog plums' in English. They are very popular in the north of Brazil. People use them to make juice and ice-cream.

tapir – a large animal with a thick neck and a rubbery snout. It eats fruit and plants. Young tapirs look like striped watermelons on legs!

tucumã palm – a palm-tree with sharp spikes growing up its trunk.

The Burning Rainforest

The Amazon rainforest is burning to the ground like a great library in flames. While travelling through the forest, I have met many people who shrug their shoulders and tell me there is nothing that can be done to prevent the destruction. But I have also met many people who won't shrug their shoulders. In courageous and inventive ways these people are striving to improve the quality of life of the Amazon people and working to sustain the region's extraordinary biodiversity and beauty.

One project which gives me hope is the Mamirauá Institute for Sustainable Development. This organisation manages a forest reserve to the north of Manaus which stretches for more than four thousand square miles. Until Mamirauá was created in 1990, local populations had been excluded from forest reserves in Brazil. But Mamirauá became the country's first Sustainable Development Reserve. The communities living there remain, and the institute works with the local population to improve their standard of living and to achieve sustainable use of natural resources. It is a difficult task, but I have seen the patience and enthusiasm with which the organisation goes about it.

I can only retell these stories because of the generosity I have been shown while travelling in the Amazon. To repay a little of that generosity, a percentage of the royalties from this book will go to the Mamirauá Institute for Sustainable Development.

You can find out more about the Mamirauá Institute at their website: www.mamiraua.org.br. And perhaps, one day, you will visit their reserve at the heart of the rainforest.

Sean Taylor

With warm thanks to Adriana and other helpers along the way: Regina Machado, Renata Meirelles and David Reeks in São Paulo; João de Jesus Paes Loureiro, Maria do Socorro Simões and Ana Rita Alves in Belém; Dona Monte Serrat and Dona Nina Abreu in Abaetetuba; Senhor Éfrem Galvão, Cristovam Sena, Geraldo Sirotheau, Zair Henrique Santos, Waldir Lemos and Sofia Sakaguchi in Santarém; Poeta Thiago de Mello, Joanice, Luis Carlos, Senhor Ignácio Lucas, Raimundo and Rosangela in Barreirinha; Dona Coló dos Santos, Senhor Feliz dos Santos and their family in Freguesia; Rich Sylvester, Alex Shankland and Geoffrey Court in England.